Noodle
& Lou

Liz Garton Scanlon

ILLUSTRATED BY Arthur Howard

Beach Lane Books

New York London Toronto Sydney

BEACH LANE BOOKS

An imprint of Simon & Schuster Children's Publishing Division

1230 Avenue of the Americas, New York, New York 10020

Text copyright © 2011 by Elizabeth Garton Scanlon

Illustrations copyright © 2011 by Arthur Howard

BEACH LANE BOOKS is a trademark of Simon & Schuster, Inc.

For information about special discounts for bulk purchases, please contact Simon & Schuster Special Sales at
1-866-506-1949 or business@simonandschuster.com.

The Simon & Schuster Speakers Bureau can bring authors to your live event. For more information or to book
an event, contact the Simon & Schuster Speakers Bureau at 1-866-248-3049 or visit our website at
www.simonspeakers.com.

Book design by Sonia Chaghatzbanian

The text for this book is set in Fink Heavy.

The illustrations for this book are rendered in watercolor.

Manufactured in China

1210 SCP

First Edition

10 9 8 7 6 5 4 3 2 1

Library of Congress Cataloging-in-Publication Data

Scanlon, Elizabeth Garton.

Noodle & Lou / Liz Garton Scanlon ; illustrated by Arthur Howard.–1st ed.

p. cm.

Summary: Noodle, a worm, is sad and feeling bad about himself, but his friend Lou, a bird, convinces him that
he is likeable just as he is.

ISBN 978-1-4424-0288-1 (hardcover)

[1. Self-acceptance–Fiction. 2. Friendship–Fiction. 3. Worms–Fiction. 4. Birds–Fiction.] I. Howard, Arthur, ill.

II. Title. III. Title: Noodle and Lou.

PZ8.3.S2798Noo 2011

[E]–dc22

2009042950

For C. G. C., ever my Lou

—L. G. S.

Some days don't go well, right from the start. Noodle woke up with a rain-cloudy heart.

His bright side was muddy. His high points sank low. The grass grew much greener in other worms' rows.

Some days are like this. What's a worm gonna do? Well, if he is Noodle, he'll lean on his Lou.

"My head has no eyes,"
Noodle said, feeling glum.

"So, life's a surprise!"
Lou said to his chum.

"And I don't have a beak,"
said Noodle, quite blue.

"But you're long, and so sleek, which is perfect for you!"

"But also—no feet,"
Noodle said with a shrug.

"I think you're complete." And Lou gave him a hug.

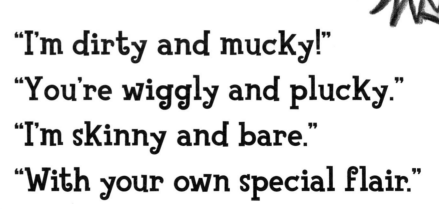

"I'm dirty and mucky!"
"You're wiggly and plucky."
"I'm skinny and bare."
"With your own special flair."

This went on for a bit,
each line like the last,
Noodle quite gloomy
and Lou just steadfast.

But Lou meant every word—
even Noodle could see.
*All those high-flyin' types,
and Lou-bird likes me!*

And in spite of himself Noodle had to admit that he and his friend were a very fine fit.

So he lifted his chin,
crawled out of his rut,
gave his sorry old slither
a jaunty new strut.

And Lou, he was tickled.
"See, you just never know,"
he said with a grin,
"how a day's gonna go."

What a worm !

*But really, thought Noodle,
the bigger surprise . . .*

is seeing yourself through your best buddy's eyes.